FUSION

GET OUTDOORS

Go Fishing!

by Meghan Gottschall

BEARPORT PUBLISHING

Minneapolis, Minnesota

President: Jen Jenson
Director of Product Development: Spencer Brinker
Senior Editor: Allison Juda
Designer: Colin O'Dea

Library of Congress Cataloging-in-Publication Data

Names: Gottschall, Meghan, author.
Title: Go fishing! / by Meghan Gottschall.
Description: Minneapolis, Minnesota : Bearport Publishing Company, [2022] |
Series: Get outdoors | Includes bibliographical references and index.
Identifiers: LCCN 2021001060 (print) | LCCN 2021001061 (ebook) | ISBN 9781647479664 (library binding) | ISBN 9781647479732 (paperback) | ISBN 9781647479800 (ebook)
Subjects: LCSH: Fishing--Juvenile literature.
Classification: LCC SH445 .G68 2022 (print) | LCC SH445 (ebook) | DDC 639.2--dc23
LC record available at https://lccn.loc.gov/2021001060
LC ebook record available at https://lccn.loc.gov/2021001061

For more information, write to Bearport Publishing, 5357 Penn Avenue South, Minneapolis, MN 55419. Printed in the United States of America.

Image Credits

Cover, © kuroksta/Shutterstock, © OpenClipart-Vectors/Pixabay, © kyoshino/Getty Images, © PRILL/Shutterstock; 1, © Oceloti/Getty Images; 6, © Air Images/Shutterstock; 8, © Terry Vine/Getty Images; 9BL, © OpenClipart-Vectors/Pixabay; 9BL, © Chippyri/Pixabay; 9BR, © adecvatman/Shutterstock; 9T, © Shane N. Cotee/Shutterstock; 10R, © Lucian Coman/Shutterstock; 10L, © Alex Tihonovs/Shutterstock; 11, © Johner Images/Getty Images; 12R, © FedBul/Shutterstock; 12L, © Maxim Petrichuk/Shutterstock; 13, © Image Source/Getty Images; 14, © Kathrin Ziegler/Getty Images; 15, © Volodymyr TVERDOKHLIB/Shutterstock; 16B, © OpenClipart-Vectors/Pixabay; 16T, © Noel V. Baebler/Shutterstock; 17T, © Alexander Sviridov/Shutterstock; 17B, © Alexander Raths/Shutterstock; 18, © Levent Konuk/Shutterstock; 19, © Dannay/Shutterstock; 21, © Dudarev Mikhail/Shutterstock; 22, © Inti St Clair/Getty Images; 23, © nadiya_sergey/Shutterstock; Background, © Clker-Free-Vector-Images/Pixabay, © Merggy/Shutterstock, © Shirstok/Shutterstock; Design elements, © Janjf93/Pixabay, © Kaliene/Pixabay, © aliaksei kruhlenia/Shutterstock, © Colorlife/Shutterstock, © JungleOutThere/Shutterstock, © NotionPic/Shutterstock, © MyClipArtStore.com/Shutterstock, © Sudowoodo/Shutterstock

CONTENTS

A FISHING ADVENTURE

Welcome to the pond! Did you know raccoons are great at catching fish? Fishing is fun for human kids, too.

Fishing is a sport where people catch fish. People fish in water all over the world from tiny ponds, to flowing streams, to big oceans.

In some places you might need a fishing **license** to catch fish. Check before you go to see if you need one!

FISHING POLES

A fishing pole is the first thing you'll need for your trip. Pick a kid-sized pole. It will be easier to hold.

The earliest fishing poles were just sticks with strings tied on the end!

If your pole is too big, you will have trouble using it.

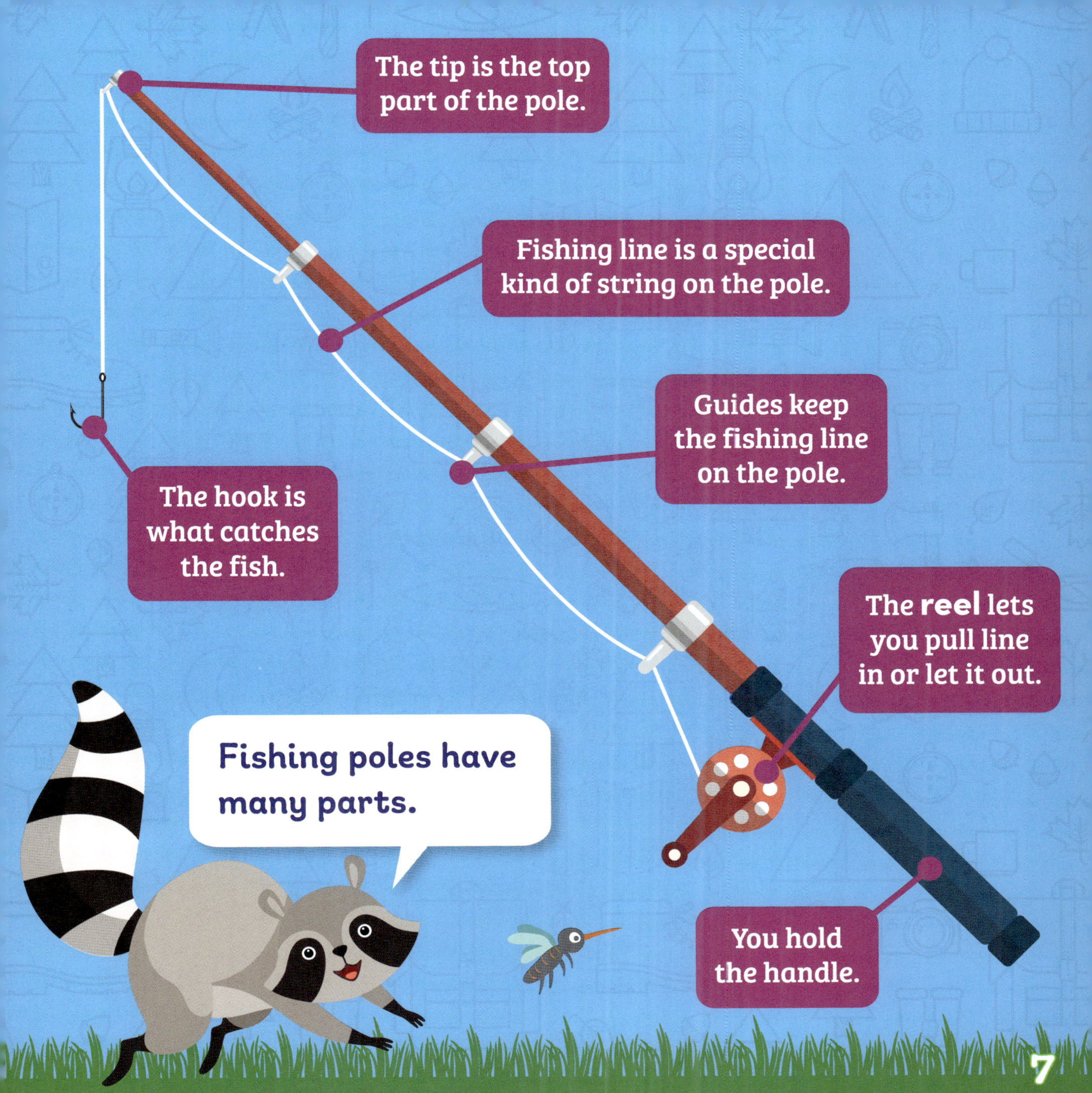
The tip is the top part of the pole.
Fishing line is a special kind of string on the pole.
Guides keep the fishing line on the pole.
The hook is what catches the fish.
The **reel** lets you pull line in or let it out.
Fishing poles have many parts.
You hold the handle.

HOOKS AND BAIT

At the end of the line on your fishing pole, you'll need a hook. When a fish bites the hook, it gets stuck. Be careful when you're adding a hook—it's very sharp!

Have an adult help you put on the hook.

Next up, it's time to add **bait**. This tasty treat will get fish to bite at your hook. Different kinds of fish eat different bait. Make sure to use bait that is just right for the fish in your area.

The bait goes right on your fishing hook.

Sometimes people use worms or crickets for bait. You can buy bait at a store or go outdoors to find your own.

ON LAND OR SEA

You've got your pole, your hook, and your bait. But where will you go? You can go anywhere that has water with fish.

Staying on land to fish is called **shore** fishing.

Some people like to fish from a boat on the water. Don't forget your life jacket!

You can go fishing all year. When the water freezes in winter, some people go ice fishing. They cut a hole in the ice to get to the water below.

Be sure to dress warmly if you go ice fishing. It's cold on a frozen lake!

CASTING

What's next? A lesson in **casting**! This is the way you get your hook and bait into the water. You can do a sidearm or overhead cast.

SIDEARM CAST

OVERHEAD CAST

Now . . . wait! **Patience** is a big part of fishing. Enjoy the outdoors while you wait for a fish to bite.

Make sure there's nothing behind you when you cast. You want to catch a fish, not a raccoon!

REELING IT IN

If you're lucky, you may feel a pull on your fishing line. You've caught a fish! Now what should you do?

The fish may pull on the line when it tries to swim away. Hold tight to your pole. When the pulling on the line stops, point your pole straight up. Turn the handle on the reel. This will pull the fish toward you.

THE BIG CATCH

It's exciting to see a fish at the end of your line. What kind did you catch?

You can catch bass from lakes and rivers. Some bass grow to more than 20 pounds (9 kg).

A sunfish may be at the end of your line if you fish in lakes or ponds. Many people think they are some of the easiest fish to catch.

There are many types of trout. Catch them by fishing in rivers, lakes, and the ocean. Most trout are about one foot (30.5 cm) long.

FOR FUN AND FOOD

Some lucky fishers put their catch on ice and take it home for dinner. It makes a fresh, tasty meal. Others don't take the fish home. When fishers put what they catch back in the water it is called catch and **release**.

Humans have been fishing for food for more than 40,000 years.

FISH FOR ALL

There are many reasons fishers catch and release. Some fish are too small. People want to give them a chance to grow bigger.

Sometimes, people catch too many fish in the same area. This is called **overfishing**. Then, other animals that eat fish don't have enough food. Putting fish back in the water means there will be plenty for animals that need them to **survive**.

GONE FISHING

Even if you don't catch a fish, you can still enjoy a day by the water. On the shore or in a boat, fishing lets you have fun outdoors with family and friends. Where will your next fishing adventure take you?

I can't wait to see you again the next time we GET OUTDOORS!

GLOSSARY

bait food used to bring an animal closer

casting throwing a fishing line into the water

license a document that gives someone permission to do something

overfishing catching too many fish in the same area

patience the ability to wait for a long time without getting upset

reel a thing that can be turned around to wind up something

release putting a fish back in the water after it is caught

shore the land along the edge of a lake, river, or ocean

survive to stay alive

INDEX